A Dragon's Purpose

Written by
Stephanie Maksymiw

Illustrated by
Children of the Tyler Robinson Foundation (TRF)

Once upon a time,
as all great stories start,
there lived an old king
in a castle falling apart.

The brick was cracked
and the rooms were drafty.
Windows were shattered
and the hallways smelled nasty.

The surrounding villagers
also had a problem.
Their crops were not growing,
there'd be no harvest this autumn.

Jacob Ramirez, age 12

The King needed a plan
before his kingdom would be lost.
But the King had no money
and it would be a great cost.

The King's trusted advisers
sat around a long table
discussing how to raise funds
when one spoke of a fable.

Megan Gifford, age 3

"Just past our realm
on a hill is a dark cave
with treasure inside
waiting for someone brave.

Diamonds and emeralds.
Coins of silver and gold.
Enough to fix this castle,
that's what I've been told.

But of course, there's a catch.
There's always one or two things.
The treasure is protected
by a dragon with wings."

Kamron Winfield, age 16

The room fell silent,
the King had to decide.
he chose the fiercest ogre
to journey up the hillside.

The ogre left the castle
ready for a fight.
He raised his fists up high
with all of his might.

The dragon was not afraid,
took a deep breath and blew
fire down at the ogre
who got scared and flew.

Jacob Ramirez, age 12

The King asked the mermaid
to be the next to try.
Her plan was to steal
all the gold she came by.

The dragon was not fooled
and noticed the thief afloat.
The dragon flung its tail
tossing her back to the castle moat.

Shaily Gonzalez, age 7

The King's last hope
was the loudest sprite.
This sprite would use her voice
to give the dragon a fright.

The dragon was not stunned
and enjoyed the noise.
The dragon decided to join in
with a roar that annoys.

Leah Gonzaga, age 10

The King now told his subjects
that they would have to be moved.
The trio had not succeeded,
the kingdom would not be improved.

Just then a young villager
grabbed her greatest possession.
She went to confront the dragon
with a little hesitation.

Megan Gifford, age 3

"I hear you like treasure,
so I've come to make a trade.
Please accept this teddy bear
in exchange for your aid."

The dragon bent down
to stare at this child,
thought for a moment
then spoke and smiled.

Gianna Burney, age 6

"Many have tried
to take my treasure.
But all have failed
after going to great measure.

They thought they were brave
when they stole, yelled, and attacked.
They did not know that kindness
can be the bravest act.

You have shown true courage,
now I am at your service.
I'll use my treasure to help,
this is a dragon's purpose."

Leah Gonzaga, age 10

The King was grateful
to have the dragon's aid.
The trio apologized
for the harm they made.

After repairs were done,
the old castle looked new.
The dragon helped to gather food
until the new crops grew.

The kingdom had been saved
by a dragon with treasure to share,
who waits for the next time
someone nicely asks for care.

Aylin Gonzales, age 8

The End

Leah Gonzaga, age 10

Thank you for purchasing this book. Proceeds from this purchase will be donated to the Tyler Robinson Foundation (TRF).

TRF is a non-profit organization established by Imagine Dragons and the Robinson Family in 2013, one month after Tyler Robinson succumbed to pediatric cancer at the age of 17. TRF honors the spirit of Tyler – his inspiring life and the positive example he had as he fought through several bouts of cancer.

Just like the dragon in this book, TRF helps those in need. The mission of TRF is to strengthen families financially and emotionally as they cope with the tragedy of a pediatric cancer diagnosis by providing grants specifically to offset out-of-pocket life expenses. More than 85% of every dollar donated goes directly to families.

All illustrations in this book were drawn by children who have been helped by TRF or whose parents work at TRF.

To learn more about TRF, visit trf.org.

If you'd like to get involved, consider becoming a TRF Ambassador where you can use your talents and creativity to raise money and awareness. To learn more about the TRF Ambassador Program, visit trf.org/ambassador.

Aisly Gonzalez, age 5

Jacob Ramirez, age 12

Benjamin Gonzalez, age 10

Leah Gonzaga, age 10

Made in the USA
Middletown, DE
29 March 2021